Level 1 is ideal for children who have received some initial reading instruction. Each story is told very simply, using a small number of frequently repeated words.

Special features:

Opening pages introduce key story words

The Ugly Duckling

Mother Duck

The eggs

The ducklings

7

6

Large, clear type

Once upon a time there were seven eggs.

Careful match between story and pictures

8

9

Educational Consultant: Geraldine Taylor
Book Banding Consultant: Kate Ruttle

A catalogue record for this book is available from the British Library

Published by Ladybird Books Ltd
80 Strand, London, WC2R 0RL
A Penguin Company

002

ISBN: 978-0-72327-263-2

Printed in China

The Ugly Duckling

Illustrated by Richard Johnson

Mother Duck

The eggs

6

The Ugly Duckling

The ducklings

Once upon a time,
there were seven eggs.

Six ducklings
were beautiful.
One duckling was not.

"You are ugly,"
said Mother Duck.

"Go away."

13

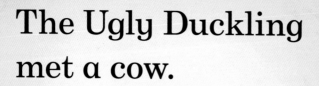

The Ugly Duckling
met a cow.

"You are ugly,"
said the cow.
"Go away."

15

The Ugly Duckling
met a cat.

"You are ugly,"
said the cat.
"Go away."

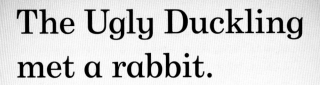

The Ugly Duckling
met a rabbit.

"You are ugly,"
said the rabbit.
"Go away."

The Ugly Duckling
met a boy.

"You are ugly,"
said the boy.
"Go away."

20

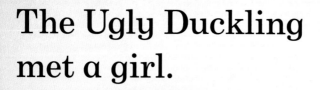

The Ugly Duckling
met a girl.

"You are ugly,"
said the girl.
"Go away."

The Ugly Duckling
was all alone.

He was very sad.

One day, the Ugly
Duckling saw some
beautiful swans.

"Look in the water,"
said the swans.

"You are beautiful,"
said the swans.
"Come with us."

And he did.

How much do you remember about the story of The Ugly Duckling? Answer these questions and find out!

- How many eggs are there in the nest?

- What does everyone tell the Ugly Duckling to do?

- What does the Ugly Duckling see when he looks in the water?

Look at the pictures from the story and say the order they should go in.

A

B

C

D

Read it yourself with Ladybird

Tick the books you've read!

For children who are ready to take their first steps in reading.

Level 1

 The Enormous Turnip ☐

 Fairy Friends ☐

 Goldilocks and the Three Bears ☐

 Little Red Hen ☐

 The Magic Porridge Pot ☐

 Little Creatures ☐

 Recycling Fun! ☐

 The Princess and the Pea ☐

 Cinderella ☐

 Rex the Big Dinosaur ☐

 The Tale of Peter Rabbit ☐

 The Three Billy Goats Gruff ☐

 Why Giraffe has a Long Neck ☐

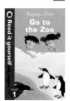 Topsy and Tim Go to the Zoo ☐

 The Ugly Duckling ☐

 The Emperor's New Clothes ☐

For beginner readers who can read short, simple sentences with help.

Level 2

 Beauty and the Beast ☐

 Chicken Licken ☐

 Little Red Riding Hood ☐

 Nature Trail ☐

 Sports Day ☐

 Pirate School ☐

 Rumpelstiltskin ☐

 Sleeping Beauty ☐

 The Gingerbread Man ☐

 Sly Fox and Red Hen ☐

 The Tale of Jemima Puddle-Duck ☐

 The Three Little Pigs ☐

 Why Lion Roarrrs! ☐

 The Big Race ☐

 Town Mouse Country Mouse ☐

 Dom's Dragon ☐

 Available on the App Store

The Read it yourself with Ladybird app is now available for iPad, iPhone and iPod touch

App also available on Android devices